The Tales of

Hunni Buny

First paperback edition December 2022

Book cover design by Meredith Woods
Illustrations by Olivia Green
Edited by Nay Merill

ISBN 979-8-218-11871-6 (paperback)

www.hunnibuntales.com

For Maxwell and Thumper:

Not even a garden full of herbs and carrots,

Nor a handful of papaya bites or bunny treats,

Could ever repay you guys for the love and companionship you give and gave.

I can't compare to the uniqueness either...

I'm just human.

Welcome to the new home of Ralph, Wes, and Hunni Bun. Hunni Bun is their adopted pet rabbit and the coolest bun ever!

Hunni Bun once lived with Countess Charlotte in the town of Duxor before meeting its new parents, Ralph and Wes.

Charlotte had got a new pet, so Hunni Bun needed a new home.

Charlotte decided to take Hunni Bun on a visit to Ralph and Wes's, and Hunni Bun moved in that same day. Now it's Hunni Bun, Ralph, Wes, and a whole new home, filled with many never-ending adventures.

Most importantly, they loved Hunni Bun bunches!!!

At the new place, Hunni Bun got to solve lots of challenges and mysteries and meet new critters from all around the world.

Today's challenge was to help Hunni Bun find its lost treasure box. Hunni Bun needed this box to get to sleep safely.

Here are three clues to help Hunni Bun.

Hunni Bun began the search in the Grand Living Room, which is Ralph and Wes's favorite place for entertainment.

Next, Hunni Bun searched the Kitchen, where a yummy smell tickled Hunni Bun's nose.

...but still no treasure.

Hunni Bun then hopped into the Great Dining Room where Ralph and Wes sit for mealtime.

No treasure for Hunni Bun here either.

Hunni Bun went to the Blue Home Office of Ralph, where he worked all day and night, according to Hunni Bun.

There were always lots of snacks to munch and crunch on; but no treasure.

High above the main level, were the Private Quarters of Ralph and Wes. They were too high for Hunni Bun to climb alone.

...but Hunni Bun found its way into the Cozy Bed Chambers with a big fancy bed fit for a king

Hunni Bun gave up searching for the lost treasure,

but then remembered there was one place left to check.

The Royal Palace of Hunni Bun, the most colorful and gigantic room ever.

That is where Hunni Bun played dress up, ate snacks, took a poop, and napped.

darker by the minute and shadows began dancing around the walls,

nto the turbulent waves and swam deeper until a bright light came from an underwater cave.

Hunni Bun sprinted into the Enchanted Closet of Wonders to sail and explore the oceans.

Hunni Bun got on board the ship and climbed up to the Crow's Nest to get a view of the entire area.

Hunni Bun checked the Captain's Quarters and ever

Hunni Bun entered the cave through the secret tunnel, and there it was, the treasure box submerged in the sand.

Hunni Bun danced with excitement and gave the box a magical smooch to reveal the lost treasure within.

Hunni Bun sprinted into the Enchanted Closet of Wonders to sail and explore the oceans.

Hunni Bun got on board the ship and climbed up to the Crow's Nest to get a view of the entire area.

Hunni Bun checked the Captain's Quarters and every deck aboard.

As the sky grew darker by the minute and shadows began dancing around the walls,

Hunni Bun dove into the turbulent waves and swam deeper until a bright light came from an underwater cave.

Hunni Bun sailed back to the Palace to return the treasure and snuggle under its soft blankie with Templeton,

but Hunni Bun was too tired.

...until next time!

Lightning Source UK Ltd.
Milton Keynes UK
UKRC031250300123
416173UK00001B/5